# You're a Bad Man, Mr Gum!

## Andy Stanton

### Illustrated by David Tazzyman

MODERN
CLASSICS

**MODERN CLASSICS**

*In memory of Sam*

First published in Great Britain 2006
This edition published 2016 by Egmont UK Limited
The Yellow Building, 1 Nicholas Road, London W11 4AN

Text Copyright © 2006 Andy Stanton
Illustrations copyright © 2006 David Tazzyman

The moral rights of the author and illustrator have been asserted

ISBN 978 1 4052 8176 8

mrgum.co.uk
www.egmont.co.uk

A CIP catalogue record for this title is available from the British Library

Printed and bound in Great Britain by the CPI Group

63301/1

Stay safe online. Any website addresses listed in this book are correct at the time of
going to print. However, Egmont is not responsible for content hosted by third parties.
Please be aware that online content can be subject to change and websites can contain
content that is unsuitable for children. We advise that all children are supervised
when using the internet

# CONTENTS

FOR
Vic

Thank you for a truly
wonderful stay. I'm
like you - I can't stand
bad reviews either. So
if you don't like this
-DON'T let me know!
All the best -

# I

# The Garden of Mr Gum

**M**r Gum was a fierce old man with a red beard and two bloodshot eyes that stared out at you like an octopus curled up in a bad cave. He was a complete horror who hated children, animals, fun and corn on the cob. What he liked was snoozing in bed all day, being lonely and scowling at things.

He slept and scowled and picked his nose and ate it. Most of the townsfolk of Lamonic Bibber avoided him and the children were terrified of him. Their mothers would say, 'Go to bed when I tell you to or Mr Gum will come and shout at your toys and leave slime on your books!' That usually did the trick.

Mr Gum lived in a great big house in the middle of town. Actually it wasn't that great, because he had turned it into a disgusting pigsty.

The rooms were filled with junk and pizza boxes. Empty milk bottles lay around like wounded soldiers in a war against milk, and there were old newspapers from years and years ago with headlines like

**VIKINGS INVADE BRITAIN**

and

**WORLD'S FIRST NEWSPAPER INVENTED TODAY.**

Insects lived in the kitchen cupboards, not just small insects but great big ones with faces and names and jobs.

Mr Gum's bedroom was absolutely grimsters. The wardrobe contained so much mould and old cheese that there was hardly any room for his moth-eaten clothes, and the bed was never made. (I don't mean that the duvet was never put back on the bed, I mean the bed had never even been MADE. Mr Gum hadn't gone to the bother of assembling it. He had just chucked all the bits of wood on the floor and dumped a mattress on top.) There was broken glass in the windows and the ancient carpet was the colour of unhappiness and smelt like a toilet. Anyway, I could be here all day going on about Mr Gum's house but I think you've got the idea. Mr Gum was an absolute lazer who couldn't be bothered with niceness and tidying and brushing his teeth, or anyone else's teeth for that matter.

(and as you can see, it's a big but) he was always extremely careful to keep his garden tidy. In fact, Mr Gum kept his garden so tidy that it was the *prettiest, greenest, flowriest, gardeniest* garden in the whole of Lamonic Bibber. Here's how amazing it was:

*Think of a number*
*between one and ten.*

*Multiply that*
*number by five.*

*Add on three*
*hundred and fifty.*

*Take away eleven.*

*Throw all those*
*numbers away.*

*Now think of an*
*amazing garden.*

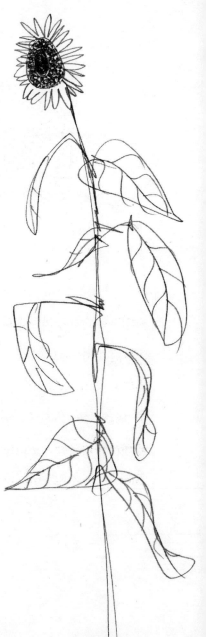

Whatever number you started with, you should now be thinking of an amazing garden. And that's how amazing Mr Gum's garden was. In spring it was bursting with crocuses and daffodils. In summer there were roses, sunflowers, and those little blue ones, what are they called again? You know, those blue ones, they look a bit like dinosaurs – anyway, there were tons of them. In autumn the leaves from the big oak tree covered the lawn, turning it gold like a gigantic leafy robot. In winter, it was winter.

No one in town could understand how Mr Gum's garden could be so *pretty, greeny, flowery* and *gardeny* when his house was such a filthy tip.

'Maybe he just likes gardening,' said Jonathan Ripples, the fattest man in town.

'Perhaps he's trying to win a garden contest,' said a little girl called Peter.

'I reckon he just quite likes gardening,' said Martin Launderette, who ran the launderette.

'Oy, that was my idea!' said Jonathan Ripples.

'No, it wasn't,' said Martin Launderette. 'You can't prove it, fatso.'

In fact, they were all wrong. The real reason was this: Mr Gum had to keep the garden tidy because otherwise an angry fairy would appear in his bathtub and start whacking him with a frying pan. (You see, there is always a simple explanation for things.) Mr Gum hated the fairy but he couldn't work out how to get rid of it, so his only choice was to do the gardening or it was pan-whacks.

And so life went on in the peaceful town of Lamonic Bibber. Everyone got on with their business and Mr Gum snoozed the days away in his dirty house and did lots of gardening he didn't want to do. And nothing much ever happened, and the sun went down over the mountains.

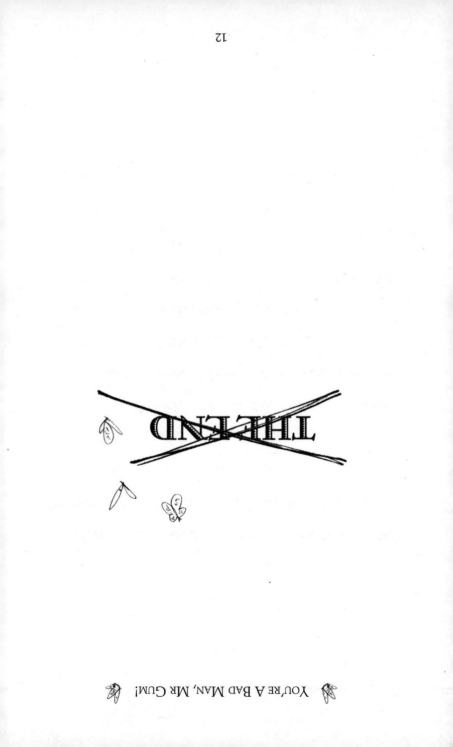

~THE END~

YOU'RE A BAD MAN, MR GUM!

*(Sorry, I nearly forgot. Something did happen once, that's what this story's about. I do apologise. Right, what was it?*

*Um . . .*

*Oh, of course! How could I be so stupid? It was that massive whopper of a dog. How on earth could I forget about <u>him</u>? Right, then.)*

One day a massive whopper of a dog –

*(Actually, I think we'd better have a new chapter. Sorry about all this, everyone.)*

## II

# A Massive Whopper
# of a Dog

One day a massive whopper of a dog came to live on the outskirts of town. Where did he come from? Nobody knows. What strange things had he seen? Nobody knows. What was his name? Everybody knows. It was Jake the dog.

He was a furry wobbler and friendly as toast and he soon made himself very popular. He would often come into town to play with the children and give them rides on his enormous broad back. No matter how many children wanted a laugh on him he never grew tired. He was just that sort of dog. If he had been a person he probably would have been a king, or at the very least a racing car driver with a cool helmet.

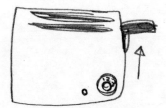

Or perhaps he would have been a gardener because Jake the dog loved nothing more than playing in gardens. He enjoyed rolling his big doggy body around on a springy green lawn to see what it felt like (generally it felt like a lawn) and chomping up the flowers in his big doggy mouth to see what they tasted like (generally they tasted like flowers). He looked so happy that nobody really minded his messy visits.

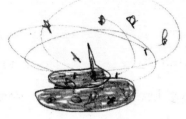

In fact, a rumour began that if Jake the dog visited your garden it meant you were in for some good luck, and if he left a 'little gift' on the lawn you were in for double good luck and maybe even a telegram from the Queen.

So the townsfolk started to leave pies and bones out on their lawns, hoping to tempt Jake into their gardens. Sometimes it worked and sometimes not. Mostly he played where he liked and when he liked. He was a free spirit, like Robin Hood or The Man in the Moon or something, I dunno – he was just a dog, after all. All summer long Jake played, and everything was fine until the fateful day he discovered a garden he'd never played in before. It was the *prettiest*, *greeniest*, *floweriest*, *gardeniest* garden in the whole of Lamonic Bibber.

On that fateful day Mr Gum was snoozing away in his unmade bed. (I told you he was a lazer and that's what lazers do.) He was dreaming his favourite dream, the one where he was a giant terrorising the townsfolk. His enormous bloodshot eyes flashed evilly like flying saucers high up in the clouds as he snatched the roofs off houses to steal the toys from the children's bedrooms. Nobody could stop him. He was the biggest and the best, he was –

# WHACK!!

For a moment Mr Gum did not know what was happening. Where were the tiny houses? Where were the frightened people? Where were the – **WHACK!!!** 'Ow!' yelled Mr Gum, rubbing his head and looking around in terror. 'Oh, no!' he rasped. The angry fairy was hovering over him, frying pan at the ready.

'Sort out the garden, you lazy snorer!' yelled the fairy, and down came the frying pan.

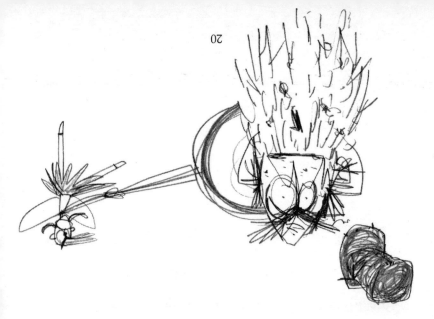

Mr Gum was too fast this time and shot out of bed like a guilty onion. **PFFF!** went the frying pan as it hit the bedcovers, sending up a little cloud of dust and ants.

Mr Gum legged it out of the bedroom and went hurtling down the stairs. He stepped on an old slice of pizza lying in the hall and skidded into the kitchen, riding it like a cheese and tomato surfboard. He could hear the fairy right behind him, shrieking with fury.

'I 'aven't done nothin' wrong! I kept the flippin' garden TIDY!' shouted Mr Gum as he flung open the back door and ran outside. He started to say something else but when he saw the garden the words got stuck in his throat.

They tasted horrible.

The garden was not tidy. The garden was a total wreck. The lawn was tuffed up and torn. The flowerbeds were trampled and chewed. Rose petals and sunflower heads lay scattered all over

the place like rose petals and sunflower heads. There was something lying under the oak tree that Mr Gum did not even want to think about. And in the centre of the wreckage played the most monstrous dog Mr Gum had ever seen.

It was Jake, of course. The beast was rolling around for his own fun, his golden-brown fur matted with grass, his happy eyes squinting into the sunshine. Before Mr Gum's disbelieving eyes, nine moles popped out of their holes and

joined the party. The two smallest ones began bouncing up and down on Jake's furry belly and doing somersaults. The rest of them chased each other in circles or had races.

**WHACK!!** The pan came down on Mr Gum's head faster than Superman. **SPLAP!!** The pan whipped him one on the bottom. A fat one to the belly. **BOING!!** Mr Gumdoubledup in pain and tripled up in fear as the fairy raged. 'It ain't my fault!'

he yelled. 'I ain't never seen that dog before!'

'I don't care whose' **BASH!** 'fault it is! It's your' **SPLURK!!** 'job to' **WALLOP!!** 'do the gardening,' **VROINNNK!!** 'you stupid trouserface!'

Mr Gum flung himself down on the lawn and lay there whimpering, his eyes shut tight in unbraveness. Jake, on the other hand, was having a brilliant time. But just then a cloud shaped a bit like a bone drifted by.

With a hungry bark Jake ran off to chase it. Mr Gum watched as the dog bounced over the fence and disappeared off to who knows where. The moles raced back to their moleholes at the speed of moles. As suddenly as it had begun, the terror was over.

Mr Gum spent all afternoon repairing the damage. The fairy watched over him, scowling and brandishing the frying pan dangerously to hurry him on. Eventually the garden was back to normal, and with one last **WHACK** for good measure the fairy flew back to the bathtub and vanished. Mr Gum breathed a sigh of relief and went inside to find he'd missed his favourite TV show, 'Bag of Sticks', which was a picture of a bag of sticks for half an hour. (Mr Gum was the only person in the country who ever watched 'Bag of Sticks'. Everyone else turned over to watch 'Funtime with Crispy'.)

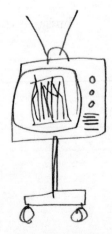

'That dog ought to be given a meddling medal, he's such a meddler,' muttered Mr Gum. 'I hope that's the last of him.'

But it wasn't the last of Jake, it was the beginning. Jake's big doggy brain could not stop thinking about that amazing garden and the very next day he returned with much the same result as before. And the day after that. And the day after that. But not the day after that, because it was a Wednesday and everyone knows that dogs have the day off on Wednesdays.

But on Thursday you should have seen him! He was back with a vengeance. Every day (apart from Wednesdays) it was the same story. That massive whopper of a dog would come bouncing over the fence and start romping around like an uncontrollable doctor, sometimes leaving his 'little gifts' as was only natural. Mr Gum would run out into the garden shaking a fist on the end of a stick to frighten him off but he could never catch him. Jake would just bark like a cheeky schoolboy doing an impression of a dog barking. Then he'd bounce over the spiky fence and disappear off to who knows where.

Three weeks later Mr Gum was covered in frying-pan-shaped bruises and he had missed ten episodes of 'Bag of Sticks'. It was time for action. Nasty action.

'It's time for action,' said Mr Gum to nobody in particular. 'Nasty action.'

Nobody in particular shrugged his shoulders and wandered off to eat his dinner. Mr Gum went to the shed and got out his thinking cap. He put it on his knee (it was a kneecap) and started thinking about how to get rid of that dog.

III

## MR GUM LAYS HIS PLANS
## LIKE THE HORROR HE IS

The next morning Mr Gum was in the butcher's shop. The butcher was a scrawny old man called Billy William the Third, and no one knew what the 'the Third' bit meant.

'I reckon he was in prison when he was younger and his number was Three,' said Jonathan Ripples, the fattest man in town.

'Maybe it's because he's the Third Nastiest Person in town,' said the little girl called Peter.

'Tell you what I think,' said Martin Launderette, who ran the launderette. 'When he was a young man, he was probably in prison and –'

'HEY!' said Jonathan Ripples. 'Stop stealing my ideas!'

'Shut up,' said Martin Launderette. 'Why don't you go on a diet?'

Of course, Billy William the Third had his own theory.

'It's cos I'm actually royalty,' he would tell anyone foolish enough to listen. 'I'm third in line for the throne of Engerland after them other geezers.' (He always pronounced 'England' in this way. Other words he said funny were 'hospital', 'fountain' and 'funny'.) Nobody believed Billy William the Third's story about being royalty except for Billy William himself, and even he didn't believe it most of the time. But he enjoyed lying. It made him laugh. Not a nice laugh like you and I would do, but a sneaky old laugh on the inside where nobody else could see.

Anyway, forget it, the important thing is that Mr Gum had gone to old BW III's butcher shop (which was called 'Billy William the Third's

Right Royal Meats') to buy the biggest load of meat he could get his angry hands on. He had a plan.

'I've got a plan,' he told Billy William. 'Next time that whopper dog comes a-playin' on my lawn, well, he better watch out, that's all! My plan is the best!'

'Are you gonna be layin' down all that meat, and poisoning it so when that barking fatty eats it he'll fall down dead?' guessed Billy William.

KIDNEYS
BONES
OLD SAUSAGES
TROTTERS
SPLEEN
BAG OF BLOOD
COW HEART

'Maybe I am,' said Mr Gum, a little annoyed that the butcher had guessed his plan so quickly. He had been looking forward to explaining it in detail and impressing Billy William with his cleverness and bad heart.

'Talking of bad heart,' said the butcher, 'here's three pounds of it. It's been sitting out in the sun since last Tuesday. That ought to poison him and no mistake, Mr Gum me old slipper!'

'Why did you leave it sitting out in the sun?'
said Mr Gum, taking the horrible sloppy bag from
the disgusting butcher.

'I like watching the flies go mad over it!'
laughed Billy William. 'They're funty!' (You see,
that was how he pronounced the word 'funny'.)
'It's the funtyiest sight in all of Engerland!
I laughed so hard I nearly had to go to
the hoppital!'

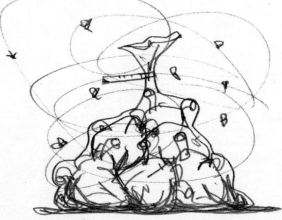

39

'Well, thank you, me old gobbler,' said Mr Gum, handing over some money that Billy William would later discover to be made out of lies and broken promises. And with that, he left the shop.

Out in the high street Mr Gum remembered he hadn't been nasty to anyone for over ten minutes. He looked around for any children who might be playing or just walking or anything, it didn't really matter what they were doing, even reading a book would be fine. Just some children he could be nasty to. But there were none to be seen so he went and bought a newspaper. He opened it up at a photo of a ten-year-old boy who'd just won the World Record Cup Reward for Secret Burping.

'This'll do nicely,' said Mr Gum, and he scowled at the photograph all the way home, hardly even looking where he was going. At one point he tripped over a stone, which made him feel like the Burper was somehow beating him, but that only made him scowl harder than ever. 'So you see, I've won again,' he said with a proud smile which he quickly turned back into a scowl.

Back home Mr Gum locked all the doors and windows, even the broken ones. Then he sat down to think on the old sailors' chest which stood in the front hall. It was a beautiful old thing made of mahogany, which is a type of wood called mahogany, and it was carved all

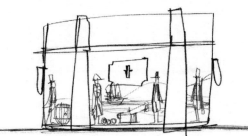

over with amazing scenes of life at sea with waves and whales and tall ships. Mr Gum had owned the sailors' chest for over forty years but he had never once taken the time to appreciate its beauty.

What's more, Mr Gum had never once thought to open that beautiful chest and see what was inside. Had he done so, it might have been a very different story indeed. It might have been *Mr Gum's Chocolatey Adventure* because I'll tell you something.

That old chest had once belonged to a sailor called Nathaniel Surname, the hero of the High Seas. One Tuesday long ago, he had saved a Spanish village from being destroyed by a terrible pirate called Kevin. As a prize, the village presented Nathaniel with the chest, which was absolutely stuffed full of chocolate. Not just any old chocolate, mind you, but special chocolate made by the dolphins of the region. And it might just be legend, but some said it was magic chocolate with

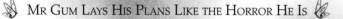 

fantastic powers, and they always whispered when they said it, which is why it is written so small.

How the chest ended up in Mr Gum's house nobody knows. But there it had stood for over forty years, unloved and unopened. As a result Mr Gum had never discovered Nathaniel's sugary treasure, which just goes to prove that angry people always miss out on their rewards. They are so busy sniping and griping that they never see the good things around them.

YOU'RE A BAD MAN, MR GUM!

As the famous song says:

*You've got to have eyes*
*Eyes for the lovely things in life!*
*If you've only got eyes*
*For the horrid and the bad*
*How you gonna get*
*I said how you gonna get*
*I said how you gonna get*
*The chocolate you deserve?*

CHORUS:
*Yeah, yeah, yeah!*
*Yeah, yeah, yeah, yeahyeahyeahyeahyeah!*
*Yeah, yeah, yeah!*
*Yes.*

You've got to have eyes
Eyes for the amazing joy and stuff!
If you've only got eyes
For old walnuts filled with spit
How you gonna get
I said how you gonna get
Tell me HOW you gonna get
The chocolate you deserve?

*(CHORUS)*

*(Guitar solo)*

*(Repeat chorus with ostrich noises to fade)*

So it was that Mr Gum found himself sitting on a sailors' fortune of what may have been magic chocolate in terrible ignorance, hatching evil.

'How do I know these cow hearts are gonna be rotten enough?' he asked himself presently. 'I'd better try eating one myself. If it kills me then I'll know it's rotten enough to use on that big woofer.'

He took out a cow's heart and opened his mouth wide.

'This is one of the craftiest things I've ever done,' he chuckled, raising the smelly greenish-

red meat to his lips. 'I am a very clever man.'

Mr Gum was just about to take a bite when he realised this might not be such a clever idea after all.

He put the heart back into the bag and thoughtfully scratched his beard, not the beard that grew on his chin but a spare one that grew on the wall that he used for scratching at from time to time.

In the end he decided to soak the rotten hearts in rat poison just to be sure. 'It can't fail!' he cackled. 'Old dogger is in for a surprise he won't like at all!'

# IV

# MR GUM HAS A CUP OF TEA

M<sup>r</sup> Gum had a cup of tea.

A

JAMMY GRAMMY LAMMY
F'HUPPA F'HUPPA BERLIN
STEREO EO LEBB C'YEPP
NERMONICA LE STRAYPEK
DE GRESPIN DE CRESPIN
DE SPESPIN DE VESPIN
DE WHOOP DE LOOP DE
BRUNKLE MERRY
CHRISTMAS LENOIR

The next morning Mr Gum inspected the cow hearts. They had been soaking all night in rat poison and they were good and proper dangerous to dogs now, and gave off a foul smell even worse than before.

*That blibberin' dog'll be smelling this bad smell and with the animal instincts of animals he'll refuse to eat 'em!* thought the crafty old man. *I'd better disguise the smell with something nice.*

Mr Gum looked through his kitchen cupboards but was there anything nice in there? Course there wasn't. All he could find was a rotten turnip, a dried-up mushroom and a sock full of stale crisps. So off he headed into town. He was in a filthy mood and as he walked along he muttered to himself. 'Shabba me whiskers,' he muttered. 'Who'd've thought poisoning that stupid whopper dog could be such hard work? What a bother it all is.'

There was a little girl playing in the hedge as Mr Gum walked by and she heard what he said and grew alarmed.

'What's old Mr Gum up to now with talk of poisoning whopper dogs?' said the little girl to herself. 'What whopper dog can he mean?' She ran through a list of all the whopper dogs that she knew. It didn't take long because she only knew one – Jake, that big loveable golden old hound.

'No!' she cried. 'No! I won't let it happen!

I loves that dog, watch out cos it's true! I loves him and what's more, that dog saved my life once and now I'm not gonna stand by playing in a hedge while that old grizzler flippin' poisons him to death and destruction! No way, says I! I'll stop him, that's what I'll do!'

Now this little girl's name was Jammy Grammy Lammy F'Huppa F'Huppa Berlin Stereo Eo Eo Lebb C'Yepp Nermonica Le Straypek De Crespin De Spespin De Vespin De

Whoop De Loop De Brunkle Merry Christmas Lenoir, but her friends just called her Polly.

You will have to make up your mind now whether or not you are her friend. If you are, then you can call her Polly too.

But if you are not, then every time you see the name 'Polly' in this story, in your head you will have to say

'Jammy Grammy Lammy F'Huppa F'Huppa
Berlin Stereo Eo Eo Lebb C'Yepp Nermonica Le
Straypek De Grespin De Crespin De Spespin De
Vespin De Whoop De Loop De Brunkle Merry
Christmas Lenoir' instead. For instance, she's
about to go running down a hill, like this:

*Polly   went   racing   down   the   hill   like   a
runaway marble.*

Now if you're her friend, then don't worry
about it. But if you're not her friend you will have

to read it like this:

*Jammy   Grammy   Lammy   F'Huppa   F'Huppa   Berlin   Stereo   Eo   Eo   Lebb   C'Yepp   Nermonica   Le   Straypek   De   Grespin   De   Crespin   De   Spespin   De   Vespin   De   Whoop   De   Loop   De   Brunkle   Merry   Christmas   Lenoir   went   racing   down   the   hill   like   a   runaway   marble.*

Most people in Lamonic Bibber chose to be Polly's friend for the sake of time and convenience.

Luckily though, Polly was a girl worth liking. She was nine years old, with lovely sandy hair like a cat's daydream and a smile as happy as the Bank of England. And when she laughed the sunlight went splashing off her pretty teeth like diamonds in search of adventure.

☆ ☆ ☆

So Polly went racing down the hill like a runaway marble, determined to find Jake the dog before he fell victim to Mr Gum's evil scheme. She didn't know exactly what the old man had in mind, but she knew her big friend was in trouble. She ran past the **Olde Curiosity Shoppe** and then ran back because she was **curious** to see what was inside. Then she remembered the danger Jake was in and continued on her way. She ran past a dustbin filled with rubbish and then another one filled with rubbish and then another one filled with rubbish and then another one filled with princesses. *Hmm, there was something unusual about one of those dustbins,* she had time to think, but she had to keep on running. She ran past big trees, little trees, tiny little trees, and tiny tiny little trees so small they were more like pebbles, in fact they were pebbles. She ran past a cat's ears which were lying on the pavement and a cat's nose and whiskers which were lying on the pavement and a cat's body and tail and legs and eyes and claws which were lying on the paveme– in fact it was all just one cat, lying on the pavement. She ran like the wind and then got tired and just walked like a breeze. But she soon sped up again because she was determined to save that tremendous dog.

It was only after she'd been running for about half an hour that she remembered something quite important: she had absolutely no idea where Jake lived. And what's more, she was no longer in Lamonic Bibber.

She had come to the woods on the edge of town and they were big and scary and full of shadows. The ancient trees looked down from on high, stern and forbidding. 'We are the trees,' they seemed to whisper. 'You are not welcome in this place. We are the trees!' A cold wind blew, making Polly shiver, and she was certain one of the flowers was snarling at her.

'Oh, no!' she cried, sitting down on one of those massive toadstools you sometimes get in spooky woods.

'I dunno where I am, an' that old Jake's facing the biggest challenge of his doggy life an' I doesn't know wheres to find him an' that flower's probbly gonna eat me!' And with that she burst into tears.

Just then an old man peered out the window of a secret cottage, half-hidden in the bushes behind her. Polly hadn't noticed the cottage and I'm sure you wouldn't have either. That's the thing about secret cottages – they're secret.

'Well, well, well,' said the old man. 'What have we here? A little girl in trouble.'

🍄 🍄 🍄

And here this chapter ends, leaving you to wonder if the old man was Mr Gum or if it was a different old man who was going to be nasty to Polly and laugh at her and stuff. Or maybe he was a good man. Yes, this chapter ends here with me not telling you that Polly was sitting outside the cottage of Friday O'Leary, a fantastic old fellow who knew the mysteries of time and space and things of that nature. And with me not telling you that he is one of the heroes

of this tale. Ha ha, I am keeping that information
to myself and you will have to wait till Chapter 7
to find it out. That is what is known as suspense.

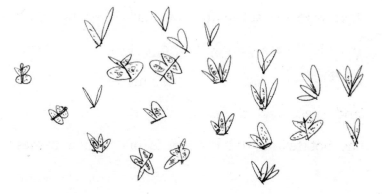

VI

# MR GUM LAYS DOWN HIS HEARTS

Meanwhile, Mr Gum was a-mumblin' and a-grumblin' his way into town. He made his way past Billy William the Third's Right Royal Meats and while he was tempted to go in, he knew that it would be a waste of time. He would never find anything nice-smelling in Billy William's butcher's shop. That was one of the reasons Mr Gum liked him. Because he was a stinker.

There were no customers with Billy William at that hour and Mr Gum could see him through the dirty window. He was playing a game of Butcher's Darts, which is exactly the same as normal darts except that the board is a pig's head and the darts are old sheep's bones. Billy William had invented it one day when he was drunk. Mr Gum loved Butcher's Darts but there was no time to pop in and challenge Billy William to a match. He had more important fish to fry. Or rather, to poison. Or rather, dog, not fish. He had more important dog to poison.

So he continued on and crossed over to Mrs Lovely's Wonderful Land of Sweets which was a sweetshop at the other end of the road. As you might guess, Mr Gum didn't enjoy going in there at all because it was a wonderland of sweets and goodness, and Mr Gum was a filthy old devil who hated good things like sweets and birthday parties and kittens dressed as clowns. He would much rather hear a piano being demolished by illegal bulldozers than a Mozart concerto. He didn't even like pop music, not even the Beatles. The only thing he liked about the Beatles was their name because they sounded like insects and you could scare people with insects. So he stepped into the sweetshop as cautiously as a paper hat in a storm. Immediately the air was full of marvellous scents. The powdery smell of sherbet lemons mingled with the odours of strawberry bombs and liquorice whips. Mr Gum felt sick. He felt as if he were being attacked by the forces of good. When he was a boy he had loved eating sweets, but that was before he

turned into a bad man. Yet now he seemed to hear the voice of the boy he had once been, calling to him down the years.

'Where did it go, all the good? Where, oh where? Turn again! Turn again! You can be good again, I know it. There is still time. Turn again, Mr Gum!' said the voice in his head.

He looked down and saw that the voice was not in his head after all, but belonged to a young boy who was standing next to him.

'Turn again, Mr Gum! You can be good again,' said the boy, offering him a fruit chew.

For some strange reason, the boy's honest face frightened Mr Gum more than anything else in that sweetshop.

'All this talk of turning again,' he snarled, shoving the boy out of the door. 'I don't like it, I tell ya. It makes me feel sick!'

At that moment Mrs Lovely came tumbling

out of the back room with her kindly eyes and kindly nose and kindly ears.

*How can noses and ears be kindly?* wondered Mr Gum, but it was true. Everything about Mrs Lovely was kindly. She was even kindly to disgraces like Mr Gum and he could not bear this. It made him want to break down inside and cry all the bad things away.

'Hello, you old witch,' he sneered. 'Give me some lemonade powder!'

Mrs Lovely's eyes sparkled. 'Yes, it is a beautiful day, Mr Gum. Yes, indeed,' she smiled as she measured out a bag of lemonade powder.

'I don't know what's so lovely about it, you old menace,' snarled Mr Gum, handing over some potatoes he had painted to look like pound coins to save money. He was annoyed to see that as soon as the potatoes touched Mrs Lovely's hands they turned into real money.

One of them turned into a jewel with a laughing face on it.

'Shabba me whiskers,' he growled, turning on his heel in disgust.

'A pleasure to see you as always, Mr Gum,' beamed Mrs Lovely as the old man stormed out with the little bag of lemonade powder clutched between his elbows. 'I do hope you come again soon.'

Mr Gum hardly noticed the walk home, mainly because he took a taxi. He couldn't wait to get his plan into action. Very soon he was back in his smelly kitchen. He rubbed his hands together gleefully and danced a cruel jig, like a spiteful imp who'd snorted over all the presents on Christmas morning. He opened the little bag and sprinkled its contents over the rotten and poisoned cow hearts. Then he gave them a quick sniff.

'Jibbers!' he gasped, clutching his throat. 'They smell of lemons and sunshine and friendship – I can hardly breathe!'

Holding it at arm's length, Mr Gum took the plate of doom out into his very neat and tidy garden. He placed it right in the middle of the lawn where Jake was sure to see it.

The day was very still. Not a single blade of grass was moving. Somewhere in the distance a chicken barked. Mr Gum settled back in his favourite broken chair and waited to see what would happen.

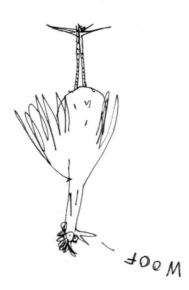

Woof

# VII

# FRIDAY O'LEARY

So now we head back to Polly, who is just where we left her, having a good old cry outside the secret cottage. Who, though, is that old man watching her from the window? You've probably been going crazy from all the suspense, haven't you? Well, you can breathe a sigh of relief because it is none other than Friday O'Leary, who is one of the heroes of this story. The next time somebody says to you, 'I hate old men. All old men are unpleasant and wicked,' don't be too quick to agree with them.

Take a minute to think about this tale.

'All old men are unpleasant and wicked? That's nonsense,' you will say.

'No, it's not,' says this somebody, whose name is Anthony, 'Mr Gum's an old man and he's a dreadful old shocker!'

'That's true, Anthony,' you say. 'And what about Billy William the Third?' says Anthony, smugly. 'He's as horrible as Brussels sprouts!'

'Well, you've got me there,' you say. 'But, Anthony, you are forgetting about Friday O'Leary. He's an old man too and he's an absolute winner!'

'Oh, I am so stupid! I forgot about Friday O'Leary,' says Anthony, 'I am going away now to pay two hundred pounds to see a glass of water balanced on a horse's back, that is how stupid I am.'

And you will never be bothered by the likes of Anthony again.

Just who was this O'Leary character, anyway? Not a lot was known about him because he was a mysterious sort of a fellow. But I will tell you what I know based on rumours, half-truths, and downright fibs:

Friday O'Leary was as old as the hills and as wise as the hills but not quite as tall as the hills. His bald head was covered in thick, curly hair and he had the normal number of legs. He was the only person ever to have found a needle in a haystack, although to be fair it was a very large needle and a tiny haystack. His favourite number was green and his favourite colour was twenty-six. He sometimes got his numbers and colours mixed up and he owned the world's smallest collection of stamps (none at all). Oh, and one last thing. Occasionally, for reasons known only to himself, Friday O'Leary shouted 'THE TRUTH IS A LEMON MERINGUE!' at the end of his sentences.

Anyway, earlier that day Friday had been sitting in his front room, playing the piano.

the truth is a lemon

He was playing a song he had written himself called 'He Was Playing a Song He Had Written Himself', all about how he was playing a song he had written himself. (He had also written a song called 'But He Wasn't Playing That at the Moment' but he wasn't playing that at the moment.)

He had just come to the final lines when the telephone rang. Friday ran to get it but he was too late because it wasn't ringing in his cottage,

Meringue

it was ringing in Ethel Frumpton's house a hundred miles away. It was her friend Mavis on the line.

'Hello, Ethel,' said Mavis. 'How's things?'

Back at the secret cottage there came the sound of crying and sobbing and general unhappy little girl noises. Friday rushed to the window and

uttered those famous, suspense-filled words I mentioned before:

'Well, well, well,' he said. 'What have we here? A little girl in trouble.'

Then he opened the front door and stepped outside.

'Hello,' he said to Polly. 'Are you all right? THE TRUTH IS A LEMON MERINGUE!'

'Who are you?' asked Polly. She was a little bit nervous because her mother had told her never to talk to strangers. Her mother was full of this sort of advice: *Brush your teeth twice a day; Wash your hands before meals; Don't cut your legs off with a breadknife.* But most of all it was *Never talk to strangers* which was blummin' good advice, especially with a stranger as strange as the stranger before her now.

'They call me Mungo Bubbles,' said the stranger, 'but I don't know why, because my name is Friday O'Leary,' and then Polly knew it was all right because her mother had told her all about this remarkable man one stormy night. This is what her mother had said:

*Friday O'Leary is a mysterious old man who lives in a secret cottage near the woods. No one knows exactly where it is, not even the Prime Minister. But if you are in dire need, you may find yourself there and he will help you with your problems. Friday O'Leary I mean, not the Prime Minister.*

Then Polly had a thought. What if it wasn't really Friday O'Leary? What if it was a bad man pretending to be him? She remembered something else her mother had told her:

*Friday O'Leary can juggle five ping pong balls and a banana, and he hardly ever drops them.*

So Polly asked the old man if he would mind juggling five

ping pong balls and a banana for her. (Luckily she had five ping pong balls and a banana in her skirt pocket.) So Friday juggled them and he hardly ever dropped them and then Polly was convinced. Suddenly the woods looked friendly and welcoming and Polly saw how beautiful all the nature was and how she probably wasn't going to be eaten by a flower or anything.

'Friday O'Leary!' she cried. 'I'm well glad to meet you! My name is Jammy Grammy Lammy F'Huppa F—'

'I think I'll just call you Polly,' said Friday.

# VIII

## SOME THINGS HAPPEN

Now I'll tell you what. Friday O'Leary wasn't the only character in this story with a mysterious house. Nobody knew where Jake the dog lived neither.

'I bet he lives on a farm and plays with all the other animals,' said Jonathan Ripples, the fattest man in town, rubbing his chins.

'Maybe he lives in the house of a rich man who feeds him bones made of gold,' said the little girl called Peter.

'This is just a guess,' said Martin Launderette. 'But perhaps he lives on a farm, where he plays with all the other ani–'

Suddenly Jonathan Ripples pounced on Martin Launderette and sat on him until he was wheezing for breath like a broken accordion.

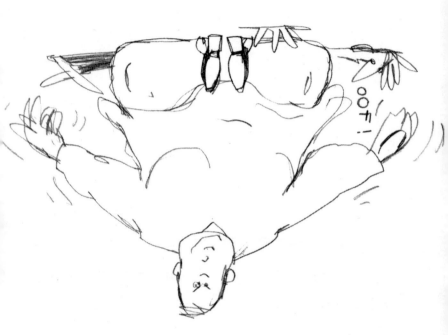

'That'll teach you not to steal people's ideas, you skinny rubbisher,' said Jonathan Ripples. 'Come on, Peter. Let's go for an ice cream.'

In any case, Jake didn't live on a farm and he didn't live in a rich man's house. Nobody knew where he lived except me, and I'm not telling you. OK – I'll tell you for a pound. OK, 50p. OK, 10p. Come on! 10p! It's not much! Oh, go on! Oh, OK, you win. I'll tell you anyway.

He lived in the woods up a horse chestnut tree. He had built a great big nest up there and filled it full of old leaves which kept him warm at night. Someone had left an old radio lying around the woods and Jake had found it one day and taken it up to his nest even though it didn't work. He was just a dog, after all.

While Polly was searching for Jake, that very dog had been having a grand old time. He'd larked around with the cuckoos, gone cuckoo with the larks and bought some tinfoil off a magpie for a couple of horse chestnuts. After lunch he decided to go into town to play in a garden or two. He shimmied down the tree quicker than you can read this sentence and set off in a very happy

mood. Off he went, strolling along in the sunshine with not a care in the world, barking and burping away and singing a song which went like this:

Bark bark bark
Bark
Baaaaaaaaaark
Bark bark bark bark
Bark bark
Woof

Soon Jake came to the town. He passed Old Granny's garden with its lovely soft lawn and pond full of friendly ducks. He passed the celebrated garden of the retired wrestler Marvellous Marvin, with its rockery in the shape of wrestling. He passed Beany McLeany's garden, where everything rhymed and the flowers grew like towers. But there was only one garden Jake fancied romping in today, and that was Mr Gum's.

On he went, on his great furry legs. Soon he came to the high street. Watching secretly from behind his greasy window, Billy William laughed to think of the nasty surprise that awaited the unsuspecting hound. 'It's funty!' he chuckled to himself as Jake walked down the road and out of sight.

— funty

At last Jake came to the spiky fence that surrounded Mr Gum's dirty house. It might have kept other dogs out. But Jake was one of those magnificent beasts who know not fear nor hesitation nor how to scramble eggs properly. He did a sort of a bouncing run and in no time a all he was over it. Well, obviously not in no time at all, of course it took *some* time. But not much. He landed in the garden in a shower of dirt and flowers, and barked his welcoming bark to let

all his garden friends know he had arrived. His welcoming bark went like this:

BARK!

As opposed to his normal bark, which went like this:

BARK!

The animals all recognised Jake's welcoming bark because it was so different from his normal one. Immediately the moles popped up out of their moleholes, the squirrels popped out of their squirrelholes, and the cats popped up out of their catholes. In Mr Gum's kitchen the toast popped out of the toaster but Mr Gum saw it trying to escape and scoffed it up greedily.

'What's going on?' he scowled – but then his eyes lit up horridly. 'I bet it's him!' he exclaimed, spitting toast everywhere. 'I bet it's that fleabag dog!'

Very carefully Mr Gum tiptoed over to the kitchen window and did secret spying with his unfriendly eyes. Outside, Jake was racing excitedly around the lawn chasing his own tail. The caterpillars were so happy to see him that they immediately metamorphosed into butterflies. One of the caterpillars was so happy that it metamorphosed into a donkey. The moles squeaked and the butterflies

roared with pleasure. The birds came swooping out the trees chirping like good 'uns and the sun seemed to do magic tricks in the sky. Mr Gum watched the whole scene unfold from behind the curtains, hating all the joy that the world was having.

'Come on, you meddler,' he said under his bad breath. 'Come on and eat them hearts.'

Then it happened. Jake suddenly stopped barking. His nose twitched as he sniffed the scent of lemonade powder. Of course, the townsfolk were always putting out delicious treats for Jake so he thought his luck was in. He bounded over to the plate of cow hearts in the middle of the lawn. The other animals froze in horror as the big dog opened his mouth. One of the moles let out a warning squeak but he only got as far as the 'squ'. It was too late. Jake's doggy jaws had already closed around a heart.

**Chew, chew, chew!** He chewed it up.

**Swallow, swallow, swallow!** He swallowed it down. **Go for another, go for another, go for another!** He went for another heart.

But before he could take another bite, he gave a sad woof and fell over on his side, his big furry belly moving rapidly in and out. Suddenly the sun was covered up by a dirty grey cloud the size of Sweden. Behind the curtains, Mr Gum was laughing like a robber.

# IX

# POLLY AND FRIDAY
# RIDE INTO TOWN

Back at the cottage Polly was telling Friday
O'Leary all about the danger Jake was
in. Friday listened carefully, saying things like
'hmm' and 'yes, I see'. Finally Polly finished her
story and looked anxiously at her new friend.

He was lost in thought, twirling an imaginary moustache which he thought made him look like a detective. Polly felt sure he was working on a brilliant plan.

'Tell me, Polly,' he said at last. 'Do you fancy a game of tennis?'

'Tennis?' said Polly. 'What about Jake?'

'Surprised exclamation! I'd forgotten all about that!' said Friday. 'There's no time to lose!'

With that he disappeared into the cottage and slammed the front door shut. Five minutes later the door was flung open again and there stood Friday dressed as a tennis player.

'Here,' he said, handing Polly a racquet. 'You can serve first because you're the guest.'

'But Mr O'Leary,' said Polly as patiently as possible. 'We've gots to save that big dog Jake like I told you millions of times just now.'

'Oh, yeah,' said Friday. 'Sorry. Let's go!'

He threw down his tennis racquet, jumped on to his motorbike, kick-started the engine and zoomed off like the devil himself. But a good devil, not an evil one.

'Hey!' shouted Polly. 'Aren't you forgetting something?'

'Oops,' said Friday, and returned to pick her up. Polly climbed into the sidecar and strapped on her helmet.

'Hold on tight! THE TRUTH IS A LEMON MERINGUE!' shouted Friday – and away they went.

It was a long ride into town. They passed hills and lakes and rivers and meadows and Scotland –

'Oops,' said Friday. 'Wrong way.'

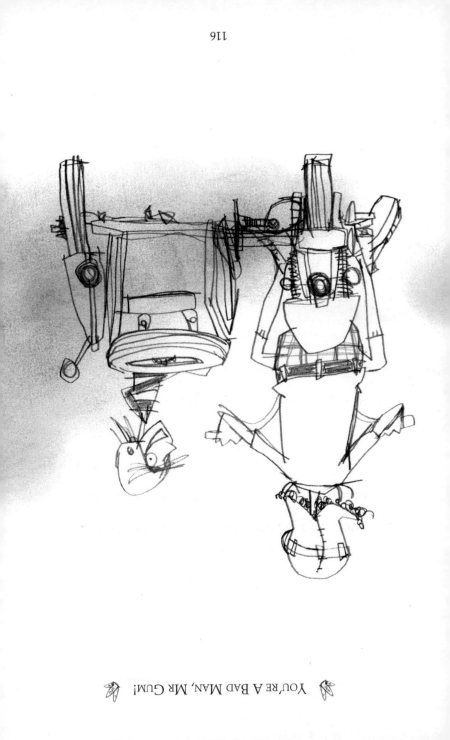

And off they belted in the opposite direction.

'Hey, Polly,' shouted Friday over the noise of the engine. 'What did you mean earlier, when you said that Jake had once saved your life?'

'How do you know I said that?' said Polly. 'There wasn't no one around when them words came out my lips.'

'It's all in this book I'm reading,' said Friday, pulling a copy of *You're A Bad Man, My Gum!* from his pocket. 'You mentioned it in Chapter 5.'

At that, Polly's face grew excited and her hair grew longer.

'Maybe it says what does gonna happen to big Jake in there!' she said.

'Don't talk of what might be in the future, little miss,' warned Friday. '"Tis unwise!

'Tis unwise!'

'Oh, please, please, let's look in that book!' said Polly. And she sounded so upset that Friday stopped the motorbike at once.

'OK,' he said, opening the book to the same page that you are reading right now. 'But **'tis unwise! 'Tis unwise!'**

No sooner had he said **"'Tis unwise,'** than Polly read those very words on the page. As Polly read about herself reading about herself the strangest feeling came over her. It felt like diving into a swimming pool full of rice in complete darkness, only the swimming pool was inside a mirror and the whole thing was a dream in someone's head. Well, it felt a bit like that, it's hard to describe.

With shaking hands Friday turned to the last chapter, only to find that the pages were completely blank.

'The future hasn't been written yet,' said Friday, starting up the bike again.

''Tis not for us to know.'

'''Twas unwise, 'twas unwise!' said Polly.

'Hey, I wanted to say that,' complained Friday, revving the engine. 'Don't steal my lines. Anyway, how did Jake save your life?'

'Oh, it was the usual sort of thing,' said Polly as they zoomed off once more. 'He rescued me from a burning centipede.'

Eventually Polly and Friday O'Leary reached town. They was a-roarin' and a-bumpin' down the high street when they were spotted by

YOU'RE A BAD MAN, MR GUM!

Billy William the Third. Knowing how Friday was a force for good, Billy William jumped out from his shop and began pegging filthy old cuts of meat in their direction.

'Ha ha!' he laughed, as Friday swerved to avoid a cascade of grey hamburgers. 'This is just like Butcher's Darts!' He picked up a bucket of tripe and sloshed it across the road. 'Take that, you force for good!' he shouted wildly.

'Hold tight, Polly!' yelled Friday as the bike went skidding in the slippery mess. 'Tripe attack!' Friday steered for his life but it was no use. The wheels got all gooed up with tripe and before you knew it he and Polly were thrown on to the pavement. They lay there helpless as Billy William advanced with a sack of kidneys.

'Is this the end?' cried Friday. 'Woe, woe is me!'

But at that moment something amazing happened. A gobstopper the size of a cannonball rolled down the street. It was quickly followed by another one even bigger than the first. Then another. All of them were hurtling with deadly accuracy towards Billy William. And they were being hurtled by none other than that wonderful seller of sweets, Mrs Lovely.

'**No!**' shouted Billy William.

In desperation, he threw a kidney at her but it missed by miles and landed in a tree. Mrs Lovely didn't bat an eyelid. On she came down the high street, humming a pretty tune about a waterfall and rolling the enormous, brightly-coloured gobstoppers before her. Soon the street was filled with them. Billy William hopped and dodged and swore like a footballer, but there were too many and down he went.

'That woman's amazing!' said Friday, his eyes shining with admiration and tripe.

'Come on, Friday! Jake needs us!' said Polly,
jumping back into the sidecar. 'Mrs Lovely can sort
this one out!'

Friday jumped back on the bike,
hit the gas and off they vammed
down the road, the battle
still raging behind them.

'I made that
happen!' said Friday
excitedly as they
gunned along.

'I magicked it so that Mrs Lovely would appear at just the right moment and save us!'

Actually he had done nothing of the sort but he wanted to keep Polly's morale up after those terrible scenes. (Also there was a tiny boastful streak in him which he couldn't help, good as he was the rest of the time.)

The two of them rode on in silence and soon they came to the high white fence that surrounded Mr Gum's garden.

# X

# JAKE'S DARKEST HOUR

Just like Jake that fence caused Polly and Friday no trouble at all. They just farted over it like blackbirds.

'More meddlers!' griped Mr Gum, dodging the angry fairy who was back with a vengeance and, of course, a frying pan. 'Who needs it?'

The motorbike screeched to a halt in front of the oak tree. Polly jumped out of the sidecar and ran up to Jake who lay on the lawn surrounded by his loyal animal friends.

The moles shook their heads sadly. A squirrel blew its nose on a butterfly. The cats looked close to tears, for Jake was the only dog they had ever loved.

Polly gasped when she saw him. The once splendid beast looked as weak as a baby. His fur had lost its shine and his eyes were rolled towards the heavens. He was a mere shadow of his former self, and his shadow was a mere shadow of his former self's shadow.

'Don't die on us, Jake!' she sobbed, throwing her arms around him. 'You're too fat and good to die!'

Jake's only reply was a feeble little woof which sounded like a door closing.

'If it hadn't been for that butcher we

could've reached him in time!' sniffed Polly.

'Time?' said Friday mysteriously. 'What is Time, little miss? **'Tis unwise** to talk of what might have been and what might have not. **'Tis unwise!'**

Polly was beginning to think that Friday was a pretty rubbish hero, but she had other things to worry about.

'What are we a-gonna do?' she wailed.

'Just you wait and everything will turn out

fine,' said Friday, tapping his nose wisely. Actually he didn't have a clue what to do but just then Mr Gum raced up, the fairy at his heels.

'It's no use, O'Leary!' cried Mr Gum, like the world's most evil seagull. 'That dog'll never bother no one again!'

'We can still saves him!' said Polly fiercely.

'I don't think so, horrible little girl,' said Mr Gum. 'Look at this.'

He pointed to his own shirt, on which was

written CHAMPION EXPERT DOG POISONER.

'That don't mean nothing,' said Polly. 'You just writ them words yourself in ketchup.'

That shut Mr Gum up for a minute because it was true.

'Hmm,' said Friday, bending down to investigate Jake even though he was secretly a bit scared of dogs. Suddenly he stood up, his imaginary detective's moustache back in all its glory.

'Tell me, Gummy me boy,' said Friday, twirling his invisible moustache cunningly. 'What is the one thing that can cure that big whopper of a dog there?'

'Why, you know as well as I do, you crazy turkey!' chuckled Mr Gum. 'The only thing what can bring a dog back from the brink is the tears of a man reunited with his long-lost brother. And that's not going to happen, now, is it?'

'Hmm,' said Friday grandly, wagging a finger like he imagined a detective would. 'The tears of a man reunited with his long-lost brother, you say? Well, guess what, Mr Gum? YOU are my long-lost brother, and I have a picture of us together when we were small, and when you grew older you went over to the dark side and became a bad man and forgot all about me, your brother, who is a force of good and now look at what you have been reduced to: poisoning a happy bouncer of a dog just to avoid a whacking from a fairy like the cowardly, bitter old thing you have become, and now that I tell you this amazing information, something inside you is bursting forth and you are filled with love and compassion and dinner and you cannot help but shed tears all over this blimmin' dog and wake it up from its terrible sleep! THE TRUTH IS A LEMON MERINGUE!'

Triumphantly, Friday handed Mr Gum a battered photograph from the old days. It showed Friday when he was but a lad, standing next to another boy.

'That other boy is you!' said Friday. 'Now bring on those tears!'

The animals gasped and Polly clapped her hands together in delight.

Mr Gum peered closely at the photo. 'Nah, that ain't me,' he said. 'We ain't long-lost brothers at all, you weirdo.'

'Oh,' said Friday. He turned to Polly miserably, his imaginary moustache drooping like an imaginary weeping willow.

'Well, little miss,' he said softly. 'I did my best.'

Suddenly it was all very quiet, like the sad bit of a story. No birds sang at that unhappy hour, no wind stirred. For once, even the angry fairy was silent. The only sound was Jake breathing in and out, weaker each time.

'Goodbye, Jake,' sniffed Polly, burying her head in his fur. 'You was a good old boy, you was.'

Just then someone tapped her on the shoulder. She looked up to see a little boy she had never seen before. Somehow, though, Polly felt as if she'd known him all her life. A feeling of great peace and warmth spread through her and –

'It's that nightmare from the sweetshop!' Mr Gum exclaimed. 'How did he get here?'

'Turn again, turn again, Mr Gum!' said the boy, with his beautiful honest face.

Mr Gum backed away, his hands raised as if to ward off a ghost.

'I don't like it one bit!' he said in a quivering voice. 'Appearing out of nowhere an' talking of turning again, I don't like it!'

'I know you can be good again,' said the boy, offering him another fruit chew.

That was enough for Mr Gum. He gave a terrified yelp, clambered over the fence and scooted off down the road, the boy's words still ringing in his ears.

The little boy turned back to Polly.

'Child,' he said, even though he was no older than she. 'Listen carefully. You must zip into Mr Gum's house and look inside the sailors' chest which stands in the front hall. It is full of magic chocolate with fantastic powers,' he whispered. 'Do not tarry but bring me as much as you can.'

Polly didn't wait to hear any more but zipped into the house. There in the hallway stood the chest. It was the only beautiful thing in that lonely place and it seemed to shine with hope and furniture polish. She threw the lid open, looked inside and found nothing at all.

The chest was completely empty.

# XI

# How It All Turned Out

It had been too long. All the chocolate had turned to dust or been eaten by sailors.

Any other girl would have given up right then and sunk to her knees in despair on Mr Gum's yuck carpet. But Polly wasn't any other girl, she was Polly.

So into the dark depths of that chest she climbed. It was much larger than it had looked from the outside and it smelt of old sea adventures and underwater business. She scrabbled around on the wooden floor, lost in the darkness, crying, hardly even remembering what she was looking for any more. She had a horrible feeling she was tarrying, even though she didn't really know what it meant.

'Well, I don't care,' she sobbed. 'I'll tarry forever if that's what it takes to saves big Jake. And what's more –'

Just then Polly's hand closed on something small, hidden right at the very back. Slowly, her heart pumping like one of those things you use to blow up balloons, she brought it into the light. On her palm lay a single chocolate in the shape of a dolphin, the very last piece of Nathaniel Surname's treasure from that Tuesday long ago.

Just once it seemed to wink at her but it could have been a trick of the light rather than a trick of the confectionery.

'You're our last hope, chocolate,' said Polly, flabbing out of the chest as fast as she could. 'I just hopes you're enough to save big Jake.'

'You have done well, child,' said the little boy when she returned. 'Now let us see if the legends are true.'

Tremblingly, Polly held Jake's jaws open and tenderly stuffed the chocolate down his gob. Just as soon as it went on his tongue it turned into a real dolphin, all silvery blue, and went sliding down his throat doing whistling noises.

For a moment nothing happened. Then Jake's eyes flickered open and he uttered a little bark. It felt good, so he did another one, a little bit louder and stronger than the first. With that second bark the day was saved and the bad stuff was at an end.

The angry fairy disappeared in a puff of blue smoke that smelt like bacon and eggs and the sun came out and started doing its magic tricks again, even better ones than before with real cards this time. The moles bounced up and down with glee and the butterflies punched their little fists into the air in triumph.

Jake got up and did a victory lap around the garden to show he was back for good. Then he did a victory lick of Polly's face with his big pink

doggy tongue until she was giggling like a werewolf.

'You are no ordinary lad,' said Friday, turning to the boy. 'Who are you really?'

'I am the Spirit of the Rainbow,' answered the boy, 'and it is my job to make the world glow with happy colours so that we can all live peacefully togeth–'

'**Spirit!**' yelled a woman's voice from next door. '**Yer tea's ready!**'

'Sorry, gotta go or my mum will kill me,' said the Spirit of the Rainbow, and off he ran for his tea.

Well, I'll tell you what. The rest of that day was brilliant. Friday and Polly marched into town on Jake's broad back and all the animals danced capers about them and a squirrel puked up from all the excitement and everyone laughed. Friday played a flute up one nostril and a trumpet up the other and all the good people of Lamonic Bibber came out and cheered and waved flags and ate feasts. (Jonathan Ripples ate an entire feast by himself and spent most of the next day in bed.)

On and on marched the joyful procession, getting bigger all the while and heading towards Mrs Lovely's Wonderful Land of Sweets.

But as they were crossing the town square, Mrs Lovely herself ran up to greet the heroes. Apart from a chicken liver hanging from one arm, the courageous woman was fully recovered from the wars against Billy William the Third.

When he saw Mrs Lovely, Friday's eyes went all shiny with admiration once again and feelings swept over him like rocketships. He got down on one knee in the middle of the town square. Then he got down on two knees. Then he got down on three knees, which hardly anyone else in the world can do. 'Mrs Lovely,' said Friday through a megaphone so everyone could hear. 'You are the best. Do you fancy getting married?'

The crowd held its breath.

A mole did a dramatic drum roll with a drum and a bread roll.

'All right,' said Mrs Lovely. 'I wasn't doing anything this weekend anyway.'

The whole town erupted with the biggest cheer yet. The butterflies rained down like confetti and Jake did a massive happy bark as if he understood exactly what was going on.

Actually he was barking at a twig he'd just noticed, but there you go. He was only a dog, after all.

'Well, that's that, then,' said Friday. 'Let's get in on the feasting action!'

But Polly had had a thought.

'Where's that old Mr Gum got to?' she said.

'He's probably off getting drunk with Billy William,' guessed Friday and he was right. That's exactly what those two were up to, hating the world and falling over from the beer.

'But do you think he'll be back?' said Polly.

Friday looked mysterious.

'Who can say what will be, little miss?' he said.

**"Tis unwise, 'tis unwise,'** said Mrs Lovely. And Friday didn't even mind that she had stolen his line because he was crazy in love and there was marrying to be done.

And so life went on in the peaceful town of
Lamonic Bibber and everyone got on with
their business. Friday married Mrs Lovely and
they invited Polly over for Sunday roasts (and
occasionally Friday did a few Sunday boasts

because of that tiny boastful streak in him, good as he was the rest of the time. But no one minded.) And Mr Gum and Billy William weren't seen for quite a while and Martin Launderette apologised to Jonathan Ripples and Jake the dog played happily in gardens all summer long. And nothing much ever happened, and the sun went down over the mountains.

# THE END

I know what you're thinking. You're thinking, *How come the story's ended but there's all these extra pages at the back? I bet there's a SECRET BONUS STORY hidden away somewhere.*

Well, forget it. The rest of these pages are just blank empty space with nothing written on them, certainly not a SECRET BONUS STORY.

So just put this book down right now. It's over. Go and hassle your mum for a biscuit or something.

Stop looking for a SECRET BONUS STORY. There isn't one, just accept it.

See? Blank empty space. That's all.

The rest of this book is just blank empty space

Blank empty space

Blank empty space

The rest of this book is just blank empty space

Tra-la-la-la-la

Are you still here? Look, I'm not going to tell you again. THERE IS NO SECRET BONUS STORY. THIS IS THE END OF THE BOOK.

THE END.

GAME OVER.

GO HOME.

BYE BYE.

# SECRET BONUS STORY!!!

# Friday O'Leary Explains the Universe

One day Polly and Friday were strolling down by the Lamonic River where the water rushes grow. It was one of them brilliant afternoons when the sun's shining and there's no school because it's burnt down or it's Saturday or something, and there's hardly any wasps around to muck things up.

'Friday,' said Polly thoughtfully. 'I'm only a little girl and that, and I don't know nothin' 'bout the Universe and stuff. Can you help me out with your wisdoms?'

'I'm glad you asked me that,' said Friday, 'because the Universe is my specialist subject and I am the winner of quizzes where that's concerned. But let us sit 'neath the apple tree in the Old Meadow yonder, for that is the best place to hear my famous teachings.'

So off they yondered to the Old Meadow and sat themselves down 'neath the apple tree and there Friday began spreading his tremendous knowledge.

'A million million years ago, before your uncle was born,' he began, 'a tiny piece of cheese was floating in the middle of Space when suddenly everything went crazy. It did a Big Bang and went flying everywhere like an old lady at a jumble sale.

'For a minute or two everything smelt of cheese. Then suddenly Planet Earth appeared because of scientific chemicals and the next thing you know a creature started growing in the sea.'

'What sort of a creature?' asked Polly.

'A grey one with teeth and a necklace,' replied Friday, nodding wisely. 'It soon got bored of just swimming around all day so it got out of the sea, shook itself off and started eating plants and dirt. One day, no one knows why, it turned into a woolly mammoth and got stuck in the ice. Then cavemen appeared, Rome fell down in an earthquake, Shakespeare invented writing and football, everyone died of the plague, a bloke discovered America under a bush and here we all are today in our Modern Times, walking about with computers up our noses.'

'I see,' said Polly. 'And what about all them other planets, like Mars and Jupiter and Venice?'

But Friday's only answer was a happy snore. For spreading knowledge is a tiring business and besides, it was very comfortable 'neath the apple tree.

As Polly walked home she thought about how lucky she was.

'Cos some children haven't got Teachers of the Universe like Friday to do wisdoms on them,' she thought. 'So how they gonna learn 'bout things properly? It's a shame, that's what I says.'

And as for the Teacher of the Universe himself, he spent the rest of the afternoon asleep in the meadow and when he woke up a horse was licking his arm.

# THE END

You're a Bad Man,
Mr Gum!

10<sup>th</sup> Anniversary Edition

**Turn the page for previously
unpublished material from the
world of Lamonic Bibber . . .**

# THE MASSIVE GIANT AND THE FLEA

Long, long ago, when Lamonic Bibber wasn't even really a town yet, just a few huts and a warlock who lived on Boaster's Hill turning turnips into balloons, there lived a massive giant. Now, this giant's name was Gavin and he really was large. His head, right, his head was so big, right, his head was so big that, well, here's the thing, right, his head was sooooo big that, OK, I hope you're ready for this, his head was soooooo ENORMOUS, right, that OK, hold on, his head was sooooooooo massive that it was about the size, are you sure you're ready for this, his head was sooooo vast that –

well, to be honest, I don't really know how big his head was.

But his hands, right, his hands were SO UNBELIEVABLY HUGE, so UNBEARABLY, INCREDIBLY COLOSSAL, right, his hands, his hands yeah, fair enough, I don't know how big his hands were either. But what about his feet? Oh my goodness! You see, Gavin the giant's feet – and I do hope you're sitting down to hear this because it really will blow your mind – well, actually I have no idea how big Gavin the giant's feet were either.

I tell you what, can we start again? The story of 'The Massive Giant And The Flea' is amazing and I want to get it exactly right.

# THE MASSIVE GIANT AND THE FLEA

Ages ago, much longer ago than you can remember because you're only about seven, Lamonic Bibber was just a few huts and also there was a warlock who I might have mentioned before who lived on Boaster's Hill turning balloons into hats. But the most incredible person in all that land was not just a person but a MASSIVE GIANT and he was called Gavin the giant.

Oh my word, he was enormous! Each one of his eyes was, well, they were just, they were, look, you know what eyes are normally like, don't you? Of course you do, you've seen eyes before. Well, the thing about these eyes of Gavin the giant's, this is what you have to understand – the thing about his eyes was, OK, look, I'm not going to lie to you, I have no idea how big Gavin the giant's eyes were, I really haven't got any idea at all. But I bet you're curious to know how big his nose was, aren't you? And if you are, then you're in for an astonishing treat, because Gavin the giant's nose, you see, Gavin the giant's nose was – OK, hold on.

Imagine a normal person's nose is about the size of an apricot, can you imagine that? Let's say that most people have a nose the size of an apricot, that's a good way to start. Now, bearing in mind that a normal person's nose is about the size of one apricot, one single, delicious apricot that you might find down the greengrocer's, or growing on a tree, actually do apricots grow on trees? Or more on bushes? I'm not sure, I know that tomatoes grow on these little kind of plants with stalks on, tomatoes are nice, aren't they?

I like tomatoes.

Anyway, here's the thing: Imagine that a normal person's nose is about the size of one apricot (or roughly three cherry tomatoes). Now, by comparison, Gavin the giant's nose was NOT the size of one apricot, it was bigger than that. How much bigger? I don't know.

Let's start again.

# The Massive Giant and the Flea

Way, way back in the distant past, Lamonic Bibber was just a few huts and a warlock who lived on Boaster's Hill, turning hats into nightingales. Now, I know this is going to surprise some of you but there was a giant who lived in those days, and I bet you can't guess his name, but it was Gavin.

Now, a lot of people, when they first hear about Gavin the giant, like you are doing now – hearing about Gavin the giant for the first time, I mean – a lot of people immediately want to know all the details. They want to know how big his head was, for example.

Or how big his hands were. Or his nose, that's quite a popular one. Which is fair enough, but I don't think that's the most amazing thing about Gavin the giant, and I'm not just saying that because I don't know the answers to all those other questions. I think the most important thing is how tall he was *overall*. I mean, at the end of the day, that is what is so impressive about giants, isn't it? How tall they are *overall*. So sit back and strap yourselves in and prepare to be amazed as I tell you how tall Gavin the giant truly was.

Right. Let's say that a normal man is about, I don't know, about as tall as – let's just say, for example, that a normal man is about as tall as a fencepost. (I know some men are slightly shorter than a fencepost, and some other men are slightly taller than a fencepost but let's just say, on average, that one man is about as tall as one fencepost.) So we can write down the following equation:

ONE MAN = ONE FENCEPOST

Now, of course, the question is this: How tall was Gavin the giant? And we can write down this question as the following equation:

GAVIN THE GIANT = ???

So. Given that a normal man is about as tall as a fencepost, and given that we don't know how tall Gavin the giant was, it is clear that Gavin the giant was quite a mysterious sort of a character. OK, so we – OK, I tell you what, this has all been a bit confusing with all these equations and things, let's start again.

# THE MASSIVE GIANT AND THE FLEA

Once upon a time there lived a giant called Gavin and one day he saw a flea.

THE END

# POLLY AND THE ANTS

One Saturday afternoon Polly was a-squishin' an' a-squashin' ants down by the riverside when Friday O'Leary happened upon the dreadful scene.

'Polly!' he exclaimed in horror. 'I thought you were a good girl!'

'Come on, Friday!' replied Polly, laughing as she jumped up and down on about twenty of the miniature creatures. 'It's just ants!'

'"Just ants"?' cried Friday. 'Little miss, you have much to learn and now is the time to start learning a bit of it. But come, let us sit 'neath the apple tree in the

Old Meadow yonder, for that is the best place to hear my famous teachings.'

So off they yondered to the Old Meadow and sat themselves down 'neath the apple tree and there Friday began spreading his tremendous knowledge like someone spreading something.

'Polly,' he began. 'I was once like you, squishing and squashing those ants 'til the cows came home. And sometimes I didn't even stop when the cows came home. A hundred ants, a thousand ants, it didn't matter to me. How I used to enjoy watching their tiny heads explode! Until, one day, I fell asleep on the riverbank and the next thing you know, in I

fell. And I was going under that murky water to my murky watery grave but guess what?'

'Dunno,' said Polly sulkily, popping an ant between her fingers and looking at all the ant juice it made.

'The ants rescued me,' said Friday solemnly. 'Even though I'd been splatting them all my young life, they forgave me and they all got into the shape of a big net and caught me and pulled me from the river, half-drowned. And they fed me sugar and leaves until I was well again and that night I met their king, who is called Big Anty and I danced with them in the moonlight and they showed me their ant treasure. So you see, it's not "just ants" after all.'

'Friday,' asked Polly, who had stopped sulking and was listening with wide eyes, even though you can't listen with eyes. 'Is that story true?'

'Everything is true, in its way,' said Friday, nodding so wisely that a spark of knowledge fell out of his ear and floated away on the wind.

Then Polly saw how bad she'd been and she sobbed to think of it.

'Friday, I been ignorant like a baby throwin' books out a window!' she said. 'I won't never again squash ants for fun, I swears I won't!'

Well, after that the two friends sat under that

apple tree and they talked and they talked until eventually it grew dark and it was home time. And as Polly trotted home she thought about Friday and about all the wisdoms he'd done on her. And here's the thing. When she got into bed that night, there was a tiny note under her pillow no bigger than a postage stamp and it said 'ThANNK yOu, POly' in funny little writing and it was signed 'B.A.' And next to it was a little piece of ant treasure. And it might have been Friday who put it there or it might have been Big Anty himself, but who knows? But from that day on Polly kept her promise and only murdered ants accidentally, and never for fun.

And what of that spark of knowledge from Friday's ear? Well, it landed on a dandelion where it was eaten by a sheep. And all that night the sheep lay awake thinking 'THE TRUTH IS A LEMON MERINGUE!' to itself, over and over until it thought it was going mad. But by dawn it was back to its normal thoughts like 'BAA' or 'TIME FOR A POO, I THINK I'LL JUST DO IT ON THE GRASS BECAUSE I HAVEN'T GOT ANY MANNERS,' and the whole thing seemed like a wonderful dream.

THE END

# About the Author

**Andy Stanton** lives in North London. He studied English at Oxford but they kicked him out. He has been a film script reader, an NHS lackey and lots of other things. He has many interests, but best of all he likes cartoons, books and music (even jazz). One day he'd like to live in New York or Berlin or one of those places because he's got fantasies of bohemia. His favourite expression is 'Oh no! My keyboard's jammed on the letter "g"'!' and his favourite word is 'gggggggggggg
ggggggggggggggggggggggggggggggggggggggggggggg
ggggggggggggggggggggggggggggggggggggggggggggg
ggggggggggggggggggggggggggggggggggggggggggggg
ggggggggggggggggggggggggggggggggggggggggggggg
ggggggggggggggggggggggggggggggggggggggggggggg
ggggggggggggggggggggggggggggggggggggggggggggg
ggggggggggggggggggggggggggggggggggggggggggggg
ggggggggggggggggggggggggggggggggggggggggggggg
ggggggggggggggggggggggggggggggggggggggggggggg
ggggggggggggggggggggggggggggggggggggggggggggg
ggggggggggggggggggggggggggggggggggggggggggggg

# About the Illustrator

**David Tazzyman** lives in South London with his girlfriend, Melanie, and their three children. He grew up in Leicester, studied illustration at Manchester Metropolitan University and then travelled around Asia for three years before moving to London in 1997. He likes football, cricket, biscuits, music and drawing. He dislikes celery.